FRAZZLED!

by Jillian Powell
illustrated by Leo Brown

FULL FLIGHT

Titles in Full Flight With Attitude

Hard Drive Boy	Jonny Zucker
Robot Safe Crackers	Jonny Zucker
Blood Wheels	Stan Cullimore
Surf Attack	Alison Hawes
The Dream Catcher	Jane A.C. West
Framed!	Jillian Powell
House of Fear	Tony Norman
Go-Kart Crazy	Roger Hurn
Spirit Tribe	Melanie Joyce
Lunar Rover	David Orme

Badger Publishing Limited
Oldmedow Road, Hardwick Industrial Estate,
King's Lynn PE30 4JJ
Telephone: 01438 791037

www.badgerlearning.co.uk

2 4 6 8 10 9 7 5 3

Framed! ISBN 978-1-84691-666-3

Series Editor: Jonny Zucker
Publisher: David Jamieson.
Editor: Danny Pearson
Design: Fi Grant
Cover illustration: Leo Brown

FRAMED!

Contents

Chapter 1
A text

"Let's go on to the next room," the tour leader said.

"Let's not!" Jason said.

The tour leader went ahead. Everyone followed.

"How many rooms are there in this castle?" Zak asked.

"About fifty, I think!" Jason said.

"Fifty? This is so boring," Zak said.

"I think I will put some music on."

He took out his MP3 player.
The tour leader glared at him.

"You can't," Jason said. "We have to take notes, remember?"

"About what?"

"I dunno. The pictures and stuff."

"Well, they are boring too!" Zak said.

"I mean, look at that one. A load of fruit and a dead cat. Who wants that on their wall?"

"It's not a cat. It's a rabbit, stupid!"
Jason said.

"Dead cat, dead rabbit. It's still boring.
Someone has even been at that peach!"
Zak said.

The tour leader glared at them again.

"This is a lovely picture," she said.
"It shows two young boys by the bridge."

"Scruffy devils!" Zak said.

"Look at this one," Jason said.
He went up to a picture.

"It's a tiger hunt. The tiger has got its teeth in the horse!"

"Ouch! Looks painful!" Zak said.

"Look at this one, Jase. It's some sort of battle."

The boys looked at the picture. Two men on horses were fighting with long poles. One had knocked the other one's head off.

"There is blood shooting out of his neck. Gross!" Zak said.

"It's a bit like that computer game, 'Death Riders!'" Jason said.

"Yeah, gross!" Zak agreed.

"As I was saying," the tour leader said, "these poor boys don't have any shoes."

"They should have worn their trainers!" Zak grinned.

Everyone turned and glared at them. Just then Zak's phone buzzed with a text.

"May I remind everyone…" the tour leader said.

She pointed to a picture. It showed a mobile phone with a cross through it.

"I'll read it in the next room." Zak said to Jason.

He went ahead.

Jason stayed with the tour group. He had spotted something. It was the biggest painting he had ever seen. It was a picture of a terrifying fire-breathing dragon. It looked as if it was flying straight at him out of the picture.

He thought that Zak would at least like this painting, so he waited a bit.

But Zak didn't come back.

Jason went into the next room. He heard something clank. He saw a suit of armour. It was moving! It opened a panel in the wall and disappeared.

"Zak, you idiot!" Jason said. "You can't scare me!"

He followed the clanking thing into a secret passage.

Chapter 2
A Battle

It was dark inside. Jason had to feel his way. He saw light ahead.

Suddenly, he was in the middle of a field. There were men and horses everywhere. A crowd was cheering and clapping.

He looked for Zak then everything went black again. Something was put over his head. It felt cold and heavy. People were dressing him. They put something on his body, then his arms, then his legs.
He tried to move. He heard clanking.

He was wearing armour!

"What are you doing?" he shouted,
but his helmet stopped the sound.

They lifted him onto a horse.

"Wait! I can't ride this thing!" Jason
shouted.

He had only been riding once. It was
pony trekking on holiday. His pony had
been the size of a large dog and very
slow.

This was a different beast. It was huge
and strong. Its sides were steaming.

Someone pushed a long pole into his
hand and slapped the horse.

It rose up. It felt like doing a wheelie on his bike. The horse charged forward. The crowd cheered.

Jason looked through the helmet. Another rider was charging towards him. He didn't look friendly.

Jason's horse went straight for him. Jason closed his eyes and held out the pole. They clashed so hard the pole almost fell out of his hand.

The crowd was going mad. Jason's horse stopped suddenly.

The other rider had come off his horse. Jason looked at him in horror. His body had no head.

A head rolled over the ground towards him. It stopped at his horse's feet. The helmet fell open. Jason froze.

It was Zak's head.

Chapter 3
In The Picture

"Oh no, what have I done?" Jason said.

"Chill, Jase!" Zak's head said.

"Watch this."

Zak's body got up and went over to his head. It picked it up and put it back on.

Zak got back on his horse.

"Bit sore but good as new!" he said.

"Oh, this is weird!" Jason said. "I must be dreaming. That tour was so boring I fell asleep!"

"No, don't you see?" Zak said. "It's that picture, the one like our computer game. Remember, the one with the blood and stuff?"

"So?"

"So, we are in the picture!"

"That is mad," Jason said. "You can't just get into a picture. I wish you could. Think about that picture in my room!"

"You mean the girl band?"

"No, the 1966 World Cup final, stupid!" Jason snapped.

"Anyway, if we are in the picture, where exactly is that?"

"I know," Zak said. "If I can get to my phone under all this kit, I can check the GPS. Here it is!"

"What does it say?" Jason said.

"It's really weird," Zak said. "It's not a map. It's just some funny name and a number."

"Well, what do we do now?" Jason said.

"Get out of here!" Zak said. "Look!"

A horse was charging towards them. Its rider looked evil.

"Quick," Jason shouted. "Ride for your life!"

Chapter 4
Tiger Hunt

"I can't see him now," Jason said at last.

"I can't see anything!" Zak said. "It's so dark in here."

They were in thick jungle.

"Where are we?" Jason said. "Try the GPS again."

Zak checked his phone.

"It's the same as before," he said. "A funny name, and some numbers."

"What numbers?"

"One, seven, six and two."

"Seventeen sixty-two!" Jason said.
"I don't like that!"

"Why?"

"Because I think it's a date. And I think
it's the date of..."

"Listen!" Zak said. "Did you hear that?
It came from behind those trees."

Suddenly, his horse took off. Zak went
flying off it.

"Quick. Get up behind me!" Jason
said. "If I am right, I think it's a..."

"Tiger!" Zak shouted.

"Exactly. We are in that tiger hunt!" Jason said. "So hurry up and get on this horse!"

Zak climbed up. He was only just in time. The tiger was right behind them. They could see its teeth.

The horse ran for its life with Jason and Zak holding on as tightly as they could.

Chapter 5
A Picnic

"Phew, that was close." Jason said. "If it hadn't seen that herd of deer we would have had it!"

The boys had come out of the jungle and were now by a river.

"Hey look, someone has left a picnic," Zak said. "Let's stop and get this armour off. I'm starving."

The boys took off the armour and sat down.

"Hey, we've got no shoes. They took our trainers," Jason said.

"Never mind that. This peach is lush."
Zak took a bite.

"That's odd," Jason said.

"What?"

"Remember the picture with the fruit?
The peach had a bite out of it. So
somewhere there is a ..."

"Dead cat!" Zak said. "I mean rabbit.
It's there, look. See the flies hanging
round?"

"Gross!" Jason said. "This is too weird. We are stuck in another picture. We have to try and get out somehow!"

"But how?" Zak said. "We don't know how we got in."

"Look! There's a boat!" Jason said. "I don't remember any boats in the pictures. Let's try that."

Chapter 6
A Boat

They got in and Zak began to row.

"Funny river," Jason said some time later. "It doesn't seem to go anywhere."

"I don't think it's a river. Maybe it's a canal?" Zak said.

"Still doesn't go anywhere. See over there?"

"Where?"

"Isn't that where we found the boat?"

"It can't be, I've been rowing for ages!" Zak said.

"Yeah, but look at the way you are rowing."

"Don't rubbish my rowing!"

"I'm not. But look, you always pull harder on the right."

"I have to, to keep the boat straight."

"Exactly. Because we are going round in circles!" Jason said. "This must be a moat. Pull over."

They pulled over and climbed up the bank.

"Great!" Zak said. "Now we are all muddy!"

At the top they saw a bridge.

"Maybe we will see more from there," Jason said.

They stood on the bridge.

"Where are we?" Zak said.

"You mean who are we?" Jason said. "Two scruffy boys, all muddy and no shoes. Remember? It's us. We are the boys in the picture."

"Not again!" Zak said. "Will we ever get out of this?"

"We have to," Jason said. "I remember the next picture. It was a dirty great dra..."

"Look!" Zak said. "Isn't that the car park over there? And there's our coach, see?"

"Result!" Jason said. "Run for it, and don't look back!"

He could almost feel the dragon's breath behind them.

The others were already on the coach.

"Where on earth have you two been?" their teacher said.

"Um...we were looking at those pictures and..."

"And we really got into them!" Zak said.